The Forest

by Kyle Mewburn
illustrated by Julie Knoblock

When Jack was a little boy,
he lived near an old forest.

Jack's dad cut down trees for the sawmill.

He used a saw with long teeth.

He used an axe, too.

The axe was very sharp.

Jack didn't like to look.

Jack's dad worked hard all day, because people needed lots of wood to make houses and paper.

Jack was scared there would be no trees left.
"Don't be scared," said his dad.

But Jack was scared.

So Jack got
some seeds.

He planted the seeds,
and watered them every day

When they were bigger,
he planted them in the forest.

Jack planted lots of seedlings, but he couldn't keep up with his dad. The forest kept getting smaller and smaller.

“It’s no good! I’ll never catch up!” said Jack.

“I’ve got an idea,” said his dad.

They made a big catapult,
and put the seeds into
some mud.
“Look at this!” said Jack’s dad

The seeds landed on the ground.

"Let's see what happens," said Jack's dad.

It took a long time
for the trees to grow.
So Jack was glad
he started planting
them when he was
a little boy.

Jack wished that
everyone had planted
as many trees as he had.

People need wood for houses and paper.
But people need forests, too.